MW00454392

Visualization Demystified

The Untold Secrets to Re-Program Your Subconscious Mind and Manifest Your Dream Reality in 5 Simple Steps

Law of Attraction Short Reads, Book 3
By Elena G. Rivers

ISBN: 978-1-80095-048-1

Legal Notice:

This book is copyright protected. It for personal use only.

Disclaimer Notice:

Please note the information contained in this document is for educational and entertainment purposes only. Every attempt has been made to provide accurate, up to date, and completely reliable information. No warranties of any kind are expressed or implied.

Readers acknowledge that the author is not engaging in the rendering of legal, financial, health, medical, or professional advice. By reading this document, the reader agrees that under no circumstances are we responsible for any losses, direct or indirect, which are incurred as a result of the use of the information contained within this document, including, but not limited to, errors, omissions, or inaccuracies.

Contents

Introduction

Are you ready to master a simple visualization process to finally manifest your desires with joy and ease while feeling more relaxed in the process?

Would you like to create a simple manifestation routine, so that you can dive deep, get rid of your fears and negative energies, and allow your dreams to come true?

Do you feel like you're too busy for overcomplicated self-development and spiritual practices, and are seeking a simple-to-follow, holistic visualization system that actually works?

If you've answered yes, to at least one of the above questions, then this book is the perfect match for the answers you've been seeking.

The good news? This simple yet highly effective visualization system works, even if you're not a visual person. It's because it consists of different layers and techniques you may pick and choose from, depending on your inner feelings and intuition.

So, don't worry if you've never visualized before, or you've attempted to visualize but never used it as a tool to manifest. I've written this book with two reader avatars in mind; Law of Attraction and visualization beginners as well as advanced manifestors who never stop learning.

So, even if you already have your own visualization system, this book will deliver some new ideas and answers you may have been seeking.

Each chapter in this book builds upon the previous one, which will allow your "visualization muscle" to develop step-by-step, so, take a few deep breaths and enjoy filling your mind with positive information.

This book is perfect for curious and ambitious souls, who love getting closer to their true, authentic selves while embracing who they really are and manifesting their dream reality from a place of love and abundance. It's also beneficial for you if you have a dream or a passion you've been working towards because it'll make your journey a lot easier!

Now, I should also mention who this book isn't for, which is always a challenging task for me. But this is what my higher self asks me to do. You see, my intention is for people to benefit from this book and use it for years to come; however, not everyone might be ready for this information.

So, I'll mention it right here in the beginning (just like I've specified in the description of this book). This book isn't for people who are looking for quick fixes and instant lottery wins. In other words: it's not for people who don't want to do the inner work.

Visualization isn't about just sitting around and waiting for something to happen. And the Law of Attraction is much more than merely winning the lottery or looking for quick ways to get large amounts of money without adding any long-term value to the world.

The mindset of "instant and superficial manifestations" often reflects the mainstream LOA, and it works very well for those who sell hype products with easy promises. *Yes, win the lottery in 7 seconds or less. You don't need to transform your energy and mindset, just buy my system!*

So, here's what I think about LOA and manifestation as well as managing your expectations. An ethical framework is critical to me.

Yea, I could definitely sell a lot more books, promising the world to you, but instead, I prefer to share the truth, because it'll help you change all areas of your life for the better and enrich you long-term.

For me, LOA and working on your ability to manifest is an equivalent to in-depth personal development and mindful repetition. It's very similar to going to the gym and nourishing your body with a healthy diet.

However, in the world of diet and fitness, there are also many shortcut programs, books, and pills and they always appeal to people who are looking for quick and short-term fixes (truth to be told, most of the time, they don't even get that quick fix they've been desperately searching for years).

But in the end, those who really succeed with health and fitness are those who take care of their bodies, get the basics right (good sleep, diet, and exercise), and truly enjoy living a healthy lifestyle.

When it comes to LOA and manifestation, it's all about working on our emotional and spiritual muscles. Some days will require deep work to make those muscles stronger, and some days will be just rest days. But even during rest days and recovery days, your manifestation muscles will be growing and benefiting from the work you've applied previously.

I see the Law of Attraction as self-development, spiritual, and healing modality. As such, it's very abundant in different tools to help you dive deeper, so that you can upgrade your mindset and energy. In other words - you can discover who you truly are, embrace your authenticity and then, take meaningful and inspired action from there.

The deeper you go and the more artificial layers you peel, the easier it will be for you to manifest your dream reality. Also, people who get started on LOA may not know what's truly good for them or what their true desires are because they're still operating from society-imposed paradigms.

For example, a person whose parents run an accounting firm may think that they want to manifest a university degree and then a successful accounting career because this is what everyone around them does, and this is what their parents want them to do.

And of course, if they genuinely want to work in accounting, then that's great! Manifesting such a goal will be authentic to them.

My accountant, for example, is very passionate about running her accounting business and helping small entrepreneurs save time so that they can focus on what they're passionate about in their companies.

And yes, she loves numbers, accounting, taxes, and all that! She enjoys being an expert in this field to help people she's passionate about helping. Her work is meaningful to her.

It was her own choice to become an accountant and start her own accounting firm because she saw a niche in the market that she wanted to serve. So, what she does is very aligned for her, and I'm incredibly grateful for her service, too, because now I know all my paper and tax work are addressed on time.

But, what if a person isn't into accounting, and they'd like to pursue something else instead? Maybe they want to open their own beauty salon? Well, since the old paradigm tells them: *hey, be an accountant like everyone in your family and have everyone love you for it,* they focus on manifesting success and a goal that isn't even theirs.

I'll be a bit repetitive with the following statement – Law of Attraction works, if you use it to manifest your own goals, not someone else's goals!

I believe that most people should focus on alignment and self-development first to learn what their true desires are *(otherwise, they'll struggle with LOA, just like I used to in my "previous life").*

At the same time, some people think that acquiring a large sum of money, fast, for example, a million dollars, will solve all their problems.

One of my acquaintances manifested nearly a million dollars winning the lottery in her home country, but it hardly solved anything for her. You see, she was manifesting from a place of lack and as a quick fix to feel better about herself (and have all her friends love her for her money, not for who she truly was).

First of all, she wasn't used to handling large amounts of money. It all starts with energy and not being afraid of having money. Good energy and feelings about money lead to motion, which is learning practical information about how to manage money or hire good money experts (accountants, tax strategists, and other specialists etc.).

Even though she was able to win the lottery, by tuning into the frequency of money, her state of being wasn't something she could keep. It was a short-term win, and the negative consequences began manifesting in her physical reality. In the words of self-development and psychology: she self-sabotaged her success.

For example, she didn't understand how taxes worked and didn't feel like consulting with a tax professional, until she was faced with a fine.

She was surprised that the personal taxes on her income took away a lot of her money. She had no idea because before winning the lottery, she worked at a minimum wage job, and her employer would pay the taxes for her.

So, she automatically assumed that if you suddenly win a large amount of money playing the lottery, you just keep it all for yourself, because she was thinking and acting from her old energy and mindset.

So, she began complaining. And, the more you complain, the more negativity you attract, so that you have more things to complain about. This is how the Universe works.

At the same time, most of her friends and family kept asking her to buy them things because they assumed it was her duty.

She felt scared of rejection, so it felt good to have the money to invite her friends out and be the queen of every party. But deep inside, she felt very empty and depressed. The money was disappearing.

After a year, she realized she had to do something because she was running out of money. She decided to invest her money, to keep generating dividends, but, once again, it was a bad investment to some shady guy, without researching the opportunity, and she lost her money and ended up in debt because of her expensive lifestyle.

Long story short, 3 years after winning the lottery, she was pretty much in the same situation she was before winning: same mindset, vibration, energy, and skillset.

After all was set and done, she acquired a limiting belief that money is bad, because of her toxic experience.

Luckily, now she's healing and recovering by focusing on manifesting happiness, self-love, and authenticity first. She's also learning about money and money management so that she's fully ready for abundance and can keep it while prospering in all areas of her life.

Another person I was blessed to meet decided to take a different path. Instead of getting fixated on winning a million dollars on a lottery and not being sure how to handle it later, she worked on her mindset, energy, vibration, and skills right from the get-go.

Her first investment in herself was to learn about self-development, life coaching, and mindset. As she was learning, she also met different people, many of whom she found very inspiring, and they shared many values. The new friends made her journey much more fun and enjoyable.

Then, she started a side business, coaching people after her 9 to 5 job or during weekends. That meant she had to stop hanging out with some old friends who just wanted to drink after work, complain, and try and hope to win the lottery or to marry a billionaire.

The Universe loves people who are proactive and radiate the energy of abundance even before they receive it. By filling your mind with positive information, and spending most of your time with people who are on the same vibration, you automatically align yourself with the higher power who has your back!

She intensively visualized her vision, one step at the time, seeking guidance from her higher self, while learning and investing in herself to become a person who could offer a quality service to the world.

When she realized her side business was making as much as her job, she quit her job to become a full-time coach and grew from there.

Every year, she would visualize a more significant impact, people she'd help, and money goal for herself and her business. In other words, she was moving on what I like to call her Visualization Ladder, step-by-step.

Today, she runs a successful 7-figure coaching company, living a life of not only freedom, success, and abundance, but also joy, fulfillment, and happiness. She loves creating products and services that help people live a better life.
Also, she was manifesting her big million-dollar vision, step-by-step. Each step had a different visualization process that she kept upgrading as she was improving her mindset, energy,

vibration, and skills (so that she could offer a high-value service to the world and manifest abundance that way).

Now, even if she lost all her money, with her mindset, energy, vibration, and skills, she'd be able to rebuild herself reasonably quickly, without desperately counting on some quick fixes.

Another tip worth mentioning is that most people misunderstand the purpose of visualization.

Visualization alone won't get you much (if anything). To be successful with visualization, you need to remember that it's only a tool that you can use to let go of your ego and overthinking, so that you can experience your dream reality in the present moment and feel like the new, 2.0 version of yourself.

There is a difference between your big vision and separate steps that get you closer to it.

One of my mentors always said: *whenever you do something; you need to know your why as well as what for*.

So, your why, is your big vision, and "what for" are different little steps that lead to it.

Visualization is a fantastic tool that can help you realize what steps you need to take, so that you can literally walk into that new vision, and act from a different paradigm.

Otherwise, you'll be doing things mindlessly, just for the sake of doing them. Yes, this week, it's visualization, and next week, some other method performed in an equally superficial manner.

You attract who you are, not what you want. Tools such as visualization can help you align your energy with your ideal reality so that you can manifest it in the physical world.

Understanding this simple piece of a puzzle will help you do anything from new energy. And there are also many benefits of visualizing which will surely motivate you to keep going.

I've been talking about it to a friend of mine who is a high-performance coach. He always says that LOA is a big woo-woo!

He was never interested in manifestation until he met me, and I began sharing my interpretation of LOA, mindset, and energy work with him. Well, he's still not into energy healing stuff, but he enjoys my mindset teachings.

We also shared our experiences with visualization, and he told me he teaches very similar stuff to his clients (such as athletes, high performers, businessmen, CEO's, and executives).

We agreed on the main benefits of visualization (even if a person is not into LOA, energy work, or manifestation):
-improved relaxation and peace of mind
-ability to increase energy naturally, almost on demand
-improved productivity and communication

It's not only about manifesting your dream reality fast. Even though I'm pretty optimistic, you'll manifest it (as long as the goals you're working on are truly yours and you are authentic), what's also exciting is your holistic self-development.

Wouldn't it be great to have a tool that's free to practice and can help you think better, work better, communicate better, sleep better, and even eat better? *(I use visualization to stick to a healthy diet, and boy does it work!).*

So, even if your goal is big, and your journey is long, manifesting the journey can also be fun, because it's the journey that will permanently raise your vibration, change your mindset, and give you new skills.

Some people try to visualize to manipulate their reality out of desperation (and so they visualize the lottery as if it was the only way, while cutting out other possibilities), and they make some short-term projections.

However, successful and wealthy people don't think that way; they envision long-term.

So do healthy people! They focus on a healthy lifestyle, not a quick diet fix to lose weight fast (and then put it back on). In other words, successful people look for long-term transformations and opportunities to upgrade their self-image, energy, mindset, and skills. Successful people never stop learning!

If you're a curious and ambitious soul with an open mind, I'm sure you'll find this publication helpful and will use it for years to come.

The real fun begins when you realize that it really works if you make it work, and so you keep upgrading your vision because what you desired a few months or years ago, is now your everyday reality. Well, never stop being grateful for what you already have; while at the same time, keep stretching and growing your manifestation and visualization muscle. Keep expanding!

What you learn will always be yours. This is what I've discovered from my ancestors, who lost everything during World War II.

They had to rebuild themselves in a different country. They always told me: *Yes, you can lose material possessions, but you can never lose your mindset, dignity, and skills!*

So, if you're ready to think long-term and manifest an extraordinary life, while living in peace, abundance, and harmony, let the journey begin!

The process in this book will work if you make it work and if the goals are indeed yours. However, even if you feel confused right now and have no idea which path to take, the visualization can help you dive deeper.

With visualization, you can find out who you are, so that you can gain clarity and then focus on manifesting it into your physical reality.

So, either way, you're good to go. You can't fail: you succeed, or you learn. Even if it takes longer for you to manifest your vision, you'll be acquiring outstanding skills while permanently shifting your vibration. Your time, effort, and investment won't be for nothing.

Ideally, you want to take 5 days, maximum a week to read this book and apply its content. Each chapter is designed for one day, and each chapter builds on a previous one.

It's important to feel your energy and mindset expand as you read through this book and do the exercises, so if you take too many breaks between each chapter, the system may not be as effective.

If you find yourself take a few days' break between the chapters, I'd recommend you start again from the beginning so that you can allow your positive energy to re-build again.

You can also read the book in one sitting if you prefer (it shouldn't take more than 2 hours, as this book is designed as a short read).

The most important part of the process (aside from this introduction, which is designed to help you manage your expectations and approach the process with the right mindset and energy), is chapter 1, which is also the longest one.

The chapters that follow aim at helping you enrich your visualization process, avoid common mistakes, and create your own visualization system you can successfully use for years to come.

Before you get started on visualizing anything, be sure to visualize through your very eyes. Don't visualize yourself from the third person as if you were watching yourself in a movie.

You want to see your dream reality through your eyes and perspective; or, in other words, from the "first-person perspective" so that you can experience it as yourself.

Free LOA Newsletter + Bonus Gift

Before we dive into the contents of this book, I'd like to offer you a free copy of my ***LOA Workbook – a powerful complimentary program (eBook & audio)*** designed to help you raise your vibration while eliminating resistance and negativity.

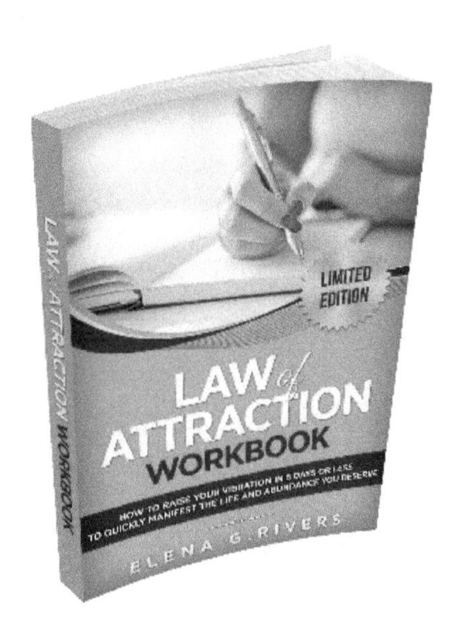

To sign up for free, visit the link below now:

www.loaforsuccess.com/newsletter

You'll also get free access to my highly acclaimed, uplifting LOA Newsletter.

Through this email newsletter, I regularly share all you need to know about the manifestation mindset and energy.

My newsletter alone helped hundreds of my readers manifest their desires.

Plus, whenever I release a new book, you can get it at a deeply discounted price or even for free.

You can also start receiving my new audiobooks published on Audible at no cost!

To sign up for free, visit the link below now:

www.loaforsuccess.com/newsletter

I'd love to connect with you and stay in touch with you while helping you on your LOA journey!

If you happen to have any technical issues with your sign up, please email us at:

support@LOAforSuccess.com

Day 1 Do You Amplify Scarcity or Abundance?

The number one lesson to keep in mind is that we visualize experiencing our dream reality in abundance. We don't visualize amplifying scarcity. It's all about staying in touch with your emotional, mental, and energetic state, not so much about how much money or success you have accumulated.

For example, I've met some wealthy people who still feel very poor, and their vibration is very low. So, even though they've manifested money, they can't enjoy abundance and vibrancy in other areas of their life.

At the same time, you'll also find wealthy and prosperous people who keep growing their health, wealth, and happiness, because they set goals and manifest from a highly vibrational emotional state.

So, this should answer the common question that people ask: *"Oh, but if a person is already successful, won't they automatically have it easier to manifest more?"*

The answer is, well, it depends on their state.
To illustrate, your state of mind or your emotional bank account isn't equivalent to your physical bank account.

I know people who are very wealthy, but they always focus on what they don't have yet, and as a result, they feel anxious or even self-sabotage their success. So, it's essential to be mindful

of your energy, and whatever your goal or dream is, keep asking yourself:
-why do I want it? (your long-term vision)

-what do I want it for? (your short-term goal, or a milestone)

-do I manifest from a place of lack or abundance?

-what do I focus on?

-do I seek to manifest my dream vision into a physical reality, because it truly is my goal? Or is it to get approval from someone, show off, or to prove someone wrong?

We always aim to manifest from pure energy, love, and a highly vibrational state!

Now, the second step in this process is developing a deep understanding between visualizing your long-term vision, and a different part of the process that leads to it.

Let's say a person wants to become a bestselling author. So, they sit all day and visualize their bestselling book written, edited, and published with a bestselling badge on it, and a ton of reviews that show appreciation for the book.

Would that alone make this vision come true, would it really happen? Of course not, because aside from the Law of Attraction, we also need to apply the law of mindful action. The word "attraction" contains the word "action" in it as well.

The process is so vital to get closer to your goals, and visualizing the process can help you increase your motivation and inspiration to stay consistent and work in alignment with your big vision.

Personally, I love to look at non-fiction authors and thought leaders I admire and use their success as my long-term inspiration. I browse through their book portfolios and "screenshot" their success in my mind, and then, I use it in my visualization. I also use it to stay on track, for example when I have a bad day. I like to sit down and visualize my end goal and remind myself that my desires already exist, not only in the quantum field but also here in our physical reality, because other people can achieve something similar! So, this is an example of long-term visualization or the end goal visualization.

One key to keep in mind though is to be very careful not to compare yourself to other people.

A comparison can result in negative feelings, not feeling worthy of success, or even jealousy. And we already know that manifesting from negative feelings doesn't lead to any pleasant circumstances and won't last.

Another example of a long-term vision would be:

A person wants to become a YouTuber or influencer. Well, they can create a list of people who have already achieved such a goal and study their work to get inspired.

They can also mentally screenshot specific images of their work and life and through visualization adopt it as their own reality.

(Please remember, you want to manifest your dreams your unique way, so don't make a mistake trying to be exactly like someone else, after all, you don't want to be someone's clone!).

One of the benefits of aligning yourself with your long-term vision is that such a practice can give you your unique answers and steps to follow, so that you can create your own process.

Then, you can devise mini visualizations for different processes or mini-goals that get you closer to your vision.

A person who wants to become a YouTuber could visualize writing down different topics they want to talk about or researching how the YouTube algorithm works or learning how to edit videos.

Visualizing the process removes resistance, so when you sit down to take mindful and inspired action on a new step, it feels like you had done it before, and so learning comes easier.

Your mind is already familiar with every new step you master, and so, there's no chance to feel anxious, worried, or not worthy of success.

Let's say you have a goal; your final goal is to go from A to E. Process visualization focuses on inserting different steps while releasing resistance.

If you attempted to go from A straight to E, you could get burned out, overwhelmed, anxious, or manifest something that doesn't last (like the person mentioned in the introduction).

Someone who gets an idea to become an inspirational speaker may want to start uploading motivational videos to YouTube to make their name known. Getting started is point A.

Now, let's say the point E for them is to be making a good living as an inspirational speaker, perhaps release a few books or programs, have coaching clients, and international speaking gigs.

If they insist on going from A straight to E, they might:

-end up comparing themselves to other people *("they can do it because they have a big YouTube channel, I'm nobody, I guess this is not for me!")*

-get overwhelmed *("it's too much work; I don't have the time now")*.

-feel upset when some troll or a negative person leaves a nasty comment ("*I'm probably not good enough!*").

However, if you visualize the process, it helps you stay focused on each step that makes you a stronger person, better manifestor, and true leader of your destiny.

It's also worth mentioning that you need coherence (created by visualizing the process steps, one by one); otherwise, you will just daydream. In other words, fluid thoughts won't materialize into tangible reality.

As you visualize the process, you get some fascinating data such as:

-limiting beliefs you may want to re-frame into positive ones (for example: *"I'm not good on camera"* can be turned to: "*Every video I make makes me a better communicator and I'm also more confident, I love the process!*")

-people and circumstances from the past that may be holding you back (for example, that class presentation in 5th grade, when someone said something mean to you, and now, you're getting a reminder to let it go so that you can focus on your new career as a motivational speaker).

-the next step to take, or a sudden idea to buy a book or a program that can help you learn the next step.

It's all like a little, coherent and holistic system where your actions, thoughts, feelings, and emotions are aligned. It's also about getting rid of the old weeds that prevent you from growing and expanding.

The action is taken, both in our minds, through visualization, as well as physically. It's mindful, inspired and entirely in alignment with your vision.

You can move with confidence, knowing that every day you're getting closer to your dream reality and becoming the new, more empowered 2.0 version of yourself. You don't even need to try and pretend. You just are! Once again, as we can see, some action is required. Law of Attraction works if you make it work.

Now, I'll add to it, miracles do happen as well, and I do believe in miracles. I always recommend my readers to be open to miracles and unexpected, positive manifestations. However, at the same time, have a long-term vision and your little manifestation roadmap that allows you to take meaningful and inspired action step-by-step.

From my personal experience, I began manifesting miracles in my life once I started taking inspired action. It's as if the Universe told me I passed the test, and it opened a new gate for me.

So yes, miracles can happen, and I highly recommend you stay open to them by visualizing the process and taking inspired action as you go! It's amazing what it can do for your vibration and overall happiness.

Some miracles may seem quite random; I've witnessed them many times, mostly in Reiki and energy work or deep healing workshops. These often take place when a person experiences a huge frequency shift.

To sum up, most of the time, I manifest by combining action and attraction. For me, it's been the most effective and pretty predictable process (if a person is willing to work it and possibly practice it several times).

I know people who daydream about becoming a millionaire, but they don't have any milestones. They want to go straight from A to Z and don't care about the process.

There's a big difference between random daydreaming and consistent visualizing. Don't get me wrong: there's nothing wrong with daydreaming. It can make you feel good and is definitely much, much better than thinking negative thoughts.

Visualization is much more than daydreaming because it automatically implies that there's some kind of a vision involved.

Now, a question I very often get asked is: *"What do I do if it doesn't work, and I waste my time on visualizing and possibly manifesting the things I didn't want anyway?"*

Well, I've briefly touched on it in the introduction, the good thing is that you can't fail, you succeed, or you learn. If you don't have a clear vision of what you want to manifest, you can use visualization as a tool to eventually help you find it. The way I see it is that you can't fail, because eventually, you'll find your true vision.

To cheer you up, if needed, personally, I had to go through the process I teach in this book several times before I began manifesting my dream reality.

It's actually thanks to what most people would label as "failures" that I was able to finally find my path and also develop the visualization system I can share with you today.

So, I highly recommend you let go of all those negative beliefs because there's nothing you can lose here. You'll come out stronger, wiser, and happier!

I can't promise you the world of instant manifestations, although these can take place if you're already very clear on what you want. If you're still not very clear on your vision, well, I was in the same place! Luckily, thanks to doing the inner work, I found my path much faster!

You see, I used to run a small marketing agency, and I wasn't passionate about it, so I was experimenting with other ventures, all of which was like an escape from my true calling and passion. In other words, I would always manifest the same pattern – chasing success, and goals that weren't even mine, to manifest money, to then feel worthy of abundance and to prove others wrong.

At first, I would visualize from a place of ego, trying out different business opportunities that everyone around me was doing.

I was acting from a scarcity mindset, and I wanted to prove my family and friends that I could make a living on my own terms.

Previously, I had quit a well-paying job to run my own business, and it served me as a vehicle to manifest a short-term financial abundance that ended up as a burnout.

But, now I'm grateful, I tested all the opportunities that did not work out, or did work out but only short term. As I was taking action (both mentally through visualization, as well as physically by testing different ventures), the voice of my intuition was getting stronger and stronger. It kept telling me to venture into the unknown and become an author while inspiring as many people as I could.

The idea was fluid; it was just a thought. I knew I had some online skills but writing books was quite challenging. In turn, I realized I needed the courage to learn, grow, and expand.

I told myself it'd be the last time I try this visualization thing. And it worked because finally, I focused on my real, love-based goal, something I was so passionate about achieving.

I knew I wanted to become an author, uplifting people through my content, following my heart, being authentic...

You see, previously, I'd get paid by influencers to create social media content for them. While, I was blessed to meet some incredible leaders and help them spread their unique message; not all my clients were fully aligned with my actual values. For example, some influencer clients I attracted at that time, were acting from a place of ego, the content they wanted seeming very superficial or even fake. Some would even request content that I thought was manipulative.

Of course, now I take responsibility for attracting people I didn't enjoy working with, because, at that time, I wasn't living in alignment and I wasn't true to myself. No wonder I would manifest people who, too, weren't authentic!

So, I didn't enjoy running such a service; it was making me feel out of balance, even though it paid well, it wasn't for me.

I knew that becoming a writer and creating my authentic content through books, content that lasts and creates a legacy, is what I wanted to focus on wholeheartedly.

However, everyone around me would tell me I couldn't make it, or some people would just laugh at my dream.

Yet I kept visualizing my goal every day (morning, evening, and whenever I needed extra energy or motivation), and I could feel my vision becoming my reality.

I kept receiving downloads from my higher Self, and these downloads contained specific instructions as to what I should check and research. Sometimes, I'd wake in in the middle of the night, inspired to do Google research on a particular topic that just popped into my mind. It was mind-blowing! I'd always take inspired action after every download.

I learned to listen to my inner voice.

Through my research, I met many successful authors who inspired me. Some of them agreed to mentor me. From there, thanks to daily visualization, I'd be presented with more incredible steps I could follow. Suddenly I could move and manifest with confidence.

I visualized the end goal (which I still do): being a serial author of countless self-help books, including the Law of Attraction, self-image, and other topics I have a passion for and knowledge/experience in. I visualized and felt gratitude coming from my beloved readers (like You!).

Suddenly there was no such thing as a writer's block everyone was talking about. Plus, even though I worked hard, it didn't feel like hard work. It felt like *inflow* work.

Each book I write is first visualized through my process visualization. For example, this week, I visualize writing, and editing this chapter. I envision attracting the perfect editor and proofreader for this book, a person who can truly heal it.

But, whenever I encounter an obstacle, for example, someone sends me a nasty email (yea, some people are in a negative place), I visualize the end goal and think of all successful authors I admire so much, so many of them left an amazing legacy for the world.

I immediately raise my vibration, and my frequency increases above the negativity. Hence, I'm no longer reactive to negative comments or remarks. If anything, I feel proactive, and they inspire me to keep doing my work mindfully, to help raise the vibration of the planet, while reducing the negativity people may feel. It's like being a part of something bigger and channeling the divine purpose!

To make this final goal exciting, I use all my senses, and I see, smell, and hear the beach where I celebrate my new book launches and take breaks from long writing sessions. I can feel the sand under my bare feet.

Then, I also visualize answering emails from my readers or authors, leaders, and bloggers I work with while enjoying a nice cup of coffee or a smoothie and listening to the sound of the ocean. I visualize the colors in the balcony I'm working from and the exact view I can admire.

So, now it's your turn. Re-model my process to your vision and goals. If you want, you can email it to me at:

elena@LOAforSuccess.com

I love helping my readers succeed! I'm also happy to give you some ideas if you get stuck and need personalized advice to help you move forward.

The process I shared in this chapter works great for me, and many others who are using it, as long as their goals and intentions are pure and truly theirs.

You need to go step-by-step. If it's too much of a stretch, the chances of manifesting it fast decrease because your mind won't believe it's possible (I'll elaborate more on that in the following chapters).

Visualization is a tool to help you stretch your mindset and emotions to make your goal familiar to you, so that you shift your self-image and take action from a new paradigm.

Ask yourself: *are you visualizing to get something fast because you're feeling lack? Or are you visualizing to experience and enjoy?*

Start with your big goal and give yourself the gift of visualizing it. Close your eyes, take a few deep breaths, and give yourself some time to see and feel all the details.

Remember to visualize everything as yourself, through your eyes. See your hands, your feet, your reflection in the mirror, your friends, your home, your work, and your bank account. Keep expanding that vision and adding more and more layers to it.

Don't worry about "the how."

The how will be unfolding as you begin visualizing the process.

However, if you're still not too sure about the process, or need more clarity on your vision, just focus on the big goal visualization.

Be creative and wholly involve your body, mind, and soul.

For example, let's say your big vision is to have a healthy and fit body. You could start visualizing yourself looking at the mirror. *How do you look, and what do you feel? Then, what do you do? Do you go to the gym in the morning? Perhaps you have a personal trainer?*

What do you eat and where do you shop?
Finally, involve different areas of your life. For example, how does your healthy body translate to your energy levels at work?

And how does your healthy lifestyle translate into your social life? What kind of people do you hang out with typically?

Likewise, if your goal is to manifest financial freedom, start visualizing yourself living your ideal lifestyle but, at the same time, incorporate other areas of life to your vision.

When you get clarity, you can start visualizing the process: that's the next step you need to take to get closer to your vision. Perhaps it's joining Pilates classes three times a week? Or investing in that forex program you've been curious about?

I call it Your Mindset Stretching routine! Do it every morning and evening to remind yourself that your big vision is safe, and your higher Self is already living abundantly and sending you guidance and instructions to follow.

Visualizing your dream regularly and adding different emotional layers to it is a fantastic mindset stretch, and it'll make you a new person, someone that knows the next step to take and moves on with clarity and confidence.

One of my business mentors always said – if you want to scale your business, first, you need to scale your mindset!

That sentence really stuck with me, and I would even add- stretch your emotions, feelings, and energy field!
Bridge the gap between your new self and your current Self by process visualization.
Once again, the right process will come when you visualize your final goal, and that goal is truly yours. For that to happen, you need the unity of heart and mind.

See the end goal to experience its vibration in the present moment. Then keep that feeling as you visualize the process and take inspired action on that process.

For example, right now, as I'm writing I feel the same vibration as I experience when I visualize my big goal/dream, and so, my vibration remains consistent throughout the day, my actions are aligned with it.

This process alone, when done consistently, can really turn you into a real manifestation monster!

Day 2 The Little-Known Secret to Embody Dream Reality Right Here, Right Now

This step will help you change your perception. It's very powerful!

While reading this program and applying it takes a few days, and I'm sure many things will click for you, the real transformation takes time.

The main reason for this is that most of the time, we don't know what we don't know. Only 5% of our mind is the conscious mind, while the rest operates subconsciously.

Unless we commit to a lifetime of personal development and getting rid of negative patterns and weeds, we'll probably keep running on harmful programs that aren't in alignment with our vision.

In other words, we have all experienced some traumas or negativity or got exposed to social conditioning that made us think in a certain way (consciously or unconsciously).

Once again, I found visualization to be extremely valuable because it can help us realize many negative patterns that are holding us back from living in alignment with our vision.

For example, a friend of mine, who aspires to be a motivational speaker, struggled with YouTube for years. By struggle, I mean this: she had all the "know-how," and she even hired a mentor who was a YouTube expert. But for some reason, she was never consistent with her videos. Even when she reached a milestone such as a certain number of views or comments or subscribers, she still felt scared to continue.

Finally, she learned about my *Visualization Demystified* process, and she kept visualizing her vision in detail.

Suddenly she started to receive downloads that clearly revealed a traumatic experience from the past, when, aged 5, she wanted to sing some songs to a family member, and he rudely told her to shut up and that she couldn't sing.

That negative experience made her live in fear for 3 decades! But, after that realization, she was able to clear the negative energy around this past event.

So, you might be interested in learning how to clear negative energy around some person or event that you found traumatic, and that makes you stuck in the old vibration? Well, from my experience, cord-cutting is one of the most effective and fastest ways to do so.

Even if you don't know the what, who, and when, you just feel like some negative energy is blocking you, but you don't know why, cord-cutting can also help you.

I recommend you start adding cord-cutting routines to your visualizations, whenever you feel stuck or heavy.

So, here's how you can cut cords with people, events, old timelines, feelings, objects, negative energies...whatever keeps you away from your vision!

Start by visualizing the individual, place, event, or feeling you wish to cut a cord with. Then, visualize scissors, so that you can cut the cord.

(For example, if you continuously feel a negative feeling, and it keeps coming up in your visualizations, but you don't know whether it was a person who caused it, or perhaps an event, you can visualize the feeling, give it a color, shape or form and then cut cords with it).

Begin by connecting to the energy of the Divine — or the source.

Visualize the energetic cord that connects you with the low vibration entity you want to let go.

Feel the energy that this entity is taking from you.

Now, set the intention to let go and visualize yourself cutting the cord between you and the negative entity, using imaginary scissors.

Visualize the energetic cords recoil back.

Now, feel the recovery of energy and thank the other entity for the role that they had in your life. Anchor that feeling of freedom and energy by pressing your thumb and index finger together.

To amplify this experience, you may choose to say (or think) the following words:

I now finally release all energetic cords because they no longer serve me.

I release you, and I remove me from these binds.

All cords are destroyed, across all dimensions, times, and planes, never to return.

I now banish these energetic cords and recover now all energy that was once lost.

My energy flows back to me, filling me once again with vitality and creating now a peaceful, energetic boundary of love and light.

Finish with some quiet time; you can meditate, lie down, or visualize something that makes you feel good. The main objective is to feel the energy that you have just reclaimed!

Think about it; you can now use this new, free energy, to focus on what you want and manifest it into your dream reality!

Finally, visualize yourself being cloaked in a luminescent blanket of energetic protection. Feel the blanket all over your body.

This is your new energetic boundary!

Set an intention that this boundary remains in place as you step confidently forward into your day.

As you focus on visualizing your end goal or the process, your mind might wander and take you to certain moments of your past, some pleasant and some unpleasant. There's nothing to worry about, as long as you are mindful of what is going on in your mind. Specific images, people, and circumstances may pop up, only because it's a sign you need to cut cords with them and move on.

Ask yourself:
-*What have you seen around you, were there any traumatic events that made you think in a certain way, and what meaning you put on those events?*

-*What are you escaping from? What are you hiding? Are your intentions pure?*

-*Were you in any toxic relationship?*

-*What are the most common society programs in your country or cultures, what is the safe route in your culture? Is it good for you and your vision?*

-*Is there something you believed to be right only to realize it wasn't for you?*

Keep diving deep. This emotional and spiritual peeling is the fastest way to help you manifest your dream reality through visualization.

While you should always focus on the positive, it's OK to have a look at your old negative patterns and beliefs just to let them go for good.

A limiting belief is when you want something, but your belief causes an internal struggle.

For example:

"I want to meet a loving man, but I think that all good men are taken".

"I want to start my own business, but I guess that all businesses require a lot of capital."

"I want more money, but I'm scared I'll have to pay more taxes, or maybe I'll get audited if I make too much money."

If you identify any limiting beliefs, focus on visualizing precisely the opposite!

For example, you can visualize making large sums of money, paying taxes with ease, and still enjoying a lot of money and living in peace and abundance.

Or, you can visualize meeting a gorgeous man who is single and wants to go out with you, and you focus on that feeling: *"Oh wow, there are great men who aren't taken!"*

Or, you can visualize your perfect business investor or a business that doesn't require much capital. You can envision yourself talking to your friend and saying:

"Wow, I can't believe I used to think that it was hard, but now, I have an amazing business, and I didn't need to have a lot of money to start it!"

Remember what we said in the previous chapters about giving your mind some evidence that what you want to manifest is safe? Well, visualizing the opposite of your limiting belief will help your mind feel safe and then look for new evidence, in alignment with that new, empowering belief.

Old patterns repeat themselves, and we should be grateful, because for us, LOA and lifetime self-growth people, patterns give us precious data, so that we can truly liberate ourselves from past limitations.

For example, I repeated negative patterns of trying to fit in and please others in my old jobs and then in my business ventures too. So, my professional life used to be about pleasing others while running away from my real interests and passions.

It was only when I transitioned to becoming an author that I realized:

"Wow, now I can finally be me!
I can be offering products and services I am passionate about, and as a result, help people and attract people who benefit from and value what I do. "

As a result, now I manifest bliss and happiness as well as amazing people in my life.

I enhanced that with visualization. Mindful but relentless, disciplined (yes, a bit of masculine energy here!), visualization to show my mind that what I want to do is safe. So, I got ideas, to start researching and listening to interviews with people and mentors I admired. Their success made my mind switch from *impossible and not safe,* to a *possible and safe mindset*!

Then, a new obstacle popped up. My mind kept nagging me with: "*Oh yea, they could do it, because they know this and that and you don't. So maybe your dream is not for you!"*

If that's the case and you realize that you end up comparing yourself to other people and you then feel blocked as a result, do this quick, energetic exercise:
Visualize yourself having a coffee with your role model.

(Please note, the goal of this exercise isn't about trying to manifest them into your life, although, who knows, that could happen as well. The main goal here is to get used to doing unusual and scary things and let your mind label them as "normal," so that you avoid self-sabotage).

Imagine you talk about things that you both do in your life, exactly as if you had the same experience in life and career.

Visualize you ask them questions, and they reply to you, or they tell you about the obstacles they had to overcome on their journeys.

The purpose of this exercise is to align yourself with the creative energy of people who are role models to you.
So, carry on visualizing yourself having a cup of coffee with them.

See your hands reaching out to grab your cup, see their cup of coffee as well. Imagine it's something familiar: you're just hanging out because you're into the same stuff and have a similar life path.

So, if right now, you have any insecurity about your ability to manifest your dream; don't worry, because in this visualization, you've already achieved your dream!

Now, you're merely telling your friend who's on the same path, precisely what it took and how you became successful.

Conclude by saying goodbye to your new friend and thank them for the meeting and tell them you'll see them soon!
Do this quick energy exercise whenever you feel stuck. You can also intertwine it with visualizing your big goal.

Another step to help you get rid of limiting thoughts that other people could manifest, but for some reason, you can't, is once again, visualizing the process.

After doing the energy exercise I shared above, this one should be much more fun!

In my case, I visualized the process of acquiring the skills I needed to succeed on my journey. At the same time, I felt incredible feelings such as: "*Oh wow, I'm not too old to learn, it feels great to learn, and yes, I can easily write up to 5 k words a day!*"

So, by visualizing and taking action at the same time, I began unpeeling all old limiting beliefs that I was too old to learn new things and change my career. I began associating learning new things with good, positive feelings, and mindful expansion.

One tactic I suggest you do is to thank your mind for having the limiting beliefs you may have because it's merely trying to protect you. Then, release them and let go. Holding on to old limiting beliefs is the energy of contraction. So is the energy of fear. And we want to expand!

Begin by expanding your mindset. Find a role model, a person who is doing what you desire to manifest. Study them and learn from them. Visualize yourself with them (of course, remember to stay true to your authentic self, it's not about becoming someone's clone!).

You can also visualize through their eyes. For example, a person who wants to manifest being a famous musician may think of their role model and visualize seeing their reality through their eyes. What do they see and do daily? How do they feel? Does what they do seem familiar to them?

For example, when I first got started on my author journey, even though I was passionate about writing, I found it very hard to write daily and stick to a daily word count. However, I discovered an author who was a bestseller both in fiction and non-fiction. He even had a book teaching people how to write faster and be more consistent. At first, I felt resistance because I feared I might burn out.

But then, I imagined I was him. For him, it was easy to write 1, 2, 3, even 5 k words (or more) a day. So, I imagined his reality as my own, just to get used to that feeling and make daily writing something normal to me. I asked myself if my writing muscle was as strong as my mentor's, what would I do? Would I procrastinate or complain? Of course not. I'd just sit down and write like a pro. It'd feel normal and familiar to me!

Another thing I did, I celebrated every milestone. For example, I imagined that 500 words were 5k words. I didn't force myself to crank out 5 k words a day suddenly, nor did I feel guilty because I produced only 500 words. I just imagined it was more if needed, and I celebrated and enjoyed the process. Our minds love such games because it makes them believe that change isn't only possible but also enjoyable, fun, and safe.

So, now ask yourself, what do you think and feel when you look at your role models? Do you think: *"If they can do it, then I can do it too?"* (in your own and unique way, of course, we've already mentioned we can't succeed by being someone else's clone).

Be mindful of any negative beliefs that may pop up.

Ask yourself- why do you have this belief and what's it trying to protect you from?

What would you do, how would you feel, if this belief didn't block you (close your eyes now and keep visualizing living your dream life without any limitations and embrace the feeling, physically, mentally and on a soul level).

-What emotions do you feel when you think of this negative belief?

-What would be the opposite of this limiting belief and emotion? What would you do and how would you feel?

The real quantum jump takes place when you have deep faith that you can move from the old paradigm ("I can't do this and that because...") to a new paradigm ("Yes, I know I can!").

When you change your paradigm, your past paradigm is still present, but you've simply expanded to a new one but remember the old one.

The key is to be aware of your old actions, feelings, and emotions, so that you can mindfully eliminate resistance by focusing on your new paradigm as you focus on your vision or the process.

Deep faith coming from the energy of already embodying your desire (not the energy of "just trying to believe") will help you make a real quantum leap.

Now, your individual beliefs are like little steps that can help you reinforce that leap and nourish your faith.

You create the image in your mind first, and then you step into it with your thoughts, feelings, emotions, and actions.

Assume there's a possibility already, whatever it is you want already exists in the quantum field. Also, don't resist any of your limiting beliefs, it's much more powerful just to accept them and mindfully work through them from that place.

Know and assume that what you desire will happen.

Have faith first. Then, support your faith with your beliefs and be mindful of your self-talk. For example, a person may visualize every day in the morning and feel amazing, but then, during the day, indulge in negative self-talk, therefore drastically lowering their vibration and sending out mixed signals to the Universe.

The Universe will think: *OK, so you want a reality where you're successful and happy only for half an hour a day when you do your morning ritual and visualize? But then, you're telling me you're not worthy of success. Ok, no problem, I'll keep you where you are while allowing you to feel happy for half an hour every day. Your wish is my command.*

Visualization will help you realize all your beliefs, both negative and positive. Then, it's up to you to start incorporating more positivity into your life, 24/7.

You can influence your reality, just let go of this concept of "everything is so hard." Don't dwell on the past, and don't stress about the future. The present moment embodies everything you need, stress-free!

Use visualization to make new, optimistic assumptions, and embody them, live by them.

Most people operate on negative assumptions, such as:
-To be healthy and fit, you need complicated diets.

-To start a business, you need a lot of money.

-To become a well-known artist or actor, you need to have the right connections.

-To have a well-paying career, you need to be born in a wealthy family.

-It's hard to find a man/woman who will love me for who I am, or they're already taken.

-It's not possible to make a good living and be financially secure as a writer or artist.

Promise yourself right here and right now that you'll refuse to focus on the negative. At the same time, celebrate every little step you take to get closer to your goals!

Day 3 The Feminine – Masculine Energy Balance and the Science of Letting Go to Visualize and Attract

Do you visualize getting closer to your goals, or do you sabotage your success and move farther away from them?

Do you use visualization to manipulate some results fast, all from a place of scarcity?

Are you getting too fixated on your goals and too attached to the outcome? Is it "it has to be all or nothing" kind of situation?

The key is exactly the opposite because we want to let go of the outcome. The reason why this wasn't discussed in the previous chapters is that it might have confused the reader who's new to manifestation and visualization.

As a result, I decided to make it the third step in this program. Also, the previous steps helped us to get rid of some old negative energies, and now we can create our vision from a place of the new paradigm. Hence, we have more energy to learn new concepts, such as the concept of letting go.

You see, people always ask me: *how can I visualize and let go at the same time? If I visualize my vision every day or do visualization for each step on my journey, doesn't that imply I'm attached to the result?*

Well, think of it as trying on some new clothes, just for the fun of trying them on, without any obligation to buy them. You already have a lot of fabulous clothes, everything you need, but you like fashion, and so you look at different clothes and try them on. Why not?

Now, let's dive a bit deeper to understand the balance between action and attraction, which will help you decide how and when to let go.

Your desire represents the feminine aspect, in other words, – attraction. As such, it doesn't care about the how it just keeps focusing on the goal. It's useful when you're still a long way from your goal, and you need to trick your mind and embody your reality here and now.

However, if you're very close to your dream, it's not really needed that much because you already know what to do, and your mind feels safe.

There's also intention- the masculine energy. It's the actions you take as well as your progress.

Now, you need both feminine and masculine energy.

Desire needs intention, and intention needs desire.

Desire leads to and creates intention. Pure desire creates pure intention, which gives you your manifestation roadmap and your unique steps to follow.

The problem is that most people lose their vital force and maybe they have some desire, but they can't create any intention. In other words, they lack masculine energy to take inspired action and focus on the process.

At the same time, some people lack the desire and feminine energy, so they're stuck in a futile cycle of forced and mindless action that leads to nowhere.

I've been guilty of both!

This chapter is all about understanding your desires and intentions. For example, a person wants to become a millionaire (a desire), so the first intention could be to be making 10k a month. They still dream big, but they also set micro goals and intentions.

Now, imagine a person whose desire is to be this super confident person, talking to everyone and being the center of every party. Well, how about first approaching a stranger and starting a conversation? How about improving that confidence muscle step by step?

Many people find LOA, and out of desperation, they try to win the lottery and become a millionaire overnight. What they don't realize is that if they don't change their self-image, their feelings, emotions, and also skills, they'll probably lose all their wealth (those stories happen all the time).

However, a self-made millionaire, who achieved their desire step-by-step, is a totally different person than he was when just getting started on the wealth creation journey.

Their mindset, energy, and skillset are so aligned to making money and wealth that even if something happened and they lost it all, they can always rebuild themselves. They work both with desire and intention.

The best way to let go, is to focus on the process and love the journey itself. The intention is the best way to let go and balance out your desire.

Visualization is a tool to help you align yourself with new realities while opening more doors for you.

Life is a balancing act. So, ask yourself if you need more desire or more intention?

If you already have a big goal and a vision, what would be the next step on your journey? What could get you closer?

Close your eyes and visualize your end goal first. Then, set the intention to break it down and ask for inspiration and the next steps.

As they come, keep visualizing them, and continue taking mindful action on them.

Stay in motion and enjoy the process. When you create, you also grow and expand, which is the opposite of contraction.

However, if you focus too much on your desire, but remain motionless, and don't follow your process, your body might enter a contracted state of anxiety, worry, fear, and doubt.

Your task for today is to focus on your next step. Give it a try, even if it seems weird. Take this step through your mind's eye as well as the physical reality to stay mindfully absorbed in creation and flow while avoiding negative feelings of impatience.

Chapter 4 The Reverse Engineer Method to Finally Control Your Mind and Be Powerful Without Limitations

It's time to learn to manage your state to help you speed up your manifestation journey and to manifest consistent results, not just some on and off manifestations.

That will help you move with confidence, knowing that you possess the power to expand while gradually increasing your goals.

It's time to break the scarcity cycle, where you just feel nervous about experiencing the same reality you don't like. When in scarcity, you feel contracted all the time, which is the opposite of expansion.

Most people say – *if you really want it, you'll get it*. And yes, there is some truth to it, as long as your state is well managed, for example, you don't desire too much (without intention and action).

If you want something badly, from a state of desperation, chances are the Universe will sense the imbalance coming out of your energy and will want to balance it out by giving you the opposite to what you desire.

Then, you may feel anxious and fearful, desperate to find the next shiny object to help you get out.

So how do you know if you attribute too much importance?

Well, ask yourself this question: *if you think about your desire, what do you feel? Do you feel abundance or scarcity? Are you fine with or without it?*

I remember that in my old business, I was very critical of myself and desperate to "close clients" and make money. At that time, I was transitioning from a full-time job to my own business and a marketing agency.

It was still the old me; I was out of alignment with who I was (I wasn't passionate about running a marketing agency and most of the time I'd typically attract clients I didn't enjoy working with). Yet, I kept forcing and pushing myself to sell my services and prove to my friends and family that I could make it.

I was working with the pure "hustle mentality."

While it felt a bit better than the victim mentality (where a person doesn't do anything), there are better states out there, for example, the "through me" aligned state of consciousness.

So, back then, I was very conscious of what I'd say to my clients, so I over-analyzed every word because I wanted to be perceived in a certain way.

Instead of focusing on my clients, their needs, and state of being, I was way too focused on my desires. I felt deep lack, both inside and outside. No wonder it didn't work out, and back then, life was a struggle for me, even though I could manifest more money into my life.

So, this is how I learned my lesson; and now, whenever I start a new project, I make sure I operate from a pure state while experiencing an abundance of good feelings.

Aside from visualizing, like described in the previous chapters, I focused on deep relaxation as I was doing it. Instead of separating myself from my vision, by feeling lack and "trying to manifest" from a place of scarcity, I began fusing myself with it.

At first, I was sending pretty inconsistent signals to the Universe, because I felt good only when visualizing in the morning and evening.

But, luckily, I became mindful of one thing - during the day, I'd write, learn, and research other authors while very often slipping into old patterns of thinking such as:

"I have to prove others wrong; they have to come to my author page and see I am a massive success; if that doesn't happen, it's not worth it. "

As those negative thoughts came, I immediately felt contracted, which, as we know, is the opposite of expansion and good state we need to manifest our dream reality and enjoy long-term success.

So, I had to make a very conscious decision to remind myself to relax during the day. Once again, a simple progressive relaxation or any adaptation of this technique is just perfect, and you can do it on your coffee break.

Below are some of my favorite relaxation tips for you to test out.

***Progressive Muscle Relaxation* by Edmund Jacobson**

First, find a quiet place where you won't be disturbed. You can lie on the floor, bed, yoga mat, or just recline in a chair if you prefer.

Be sure to feel comfortable - if you need, take off your shoes and loosen up your belt or tie.

Also, remove glasses.

Rest your hands in your lap or on the arms of the chair while focusing on deep relaxation.

Now, take a few deep breaths, very slowly. Feel your belly moving as you breathe in and out.

Keep breathing as you gradually focus your attention on the different areas of your body.

Your Forehead:
Mindfully squeeze the muscles in your forehead, for about 15 seconds.

Feel your muscles becoming tighter.

Now, slowly release the tension in your forehead while counting for 30 seconds.

Can you feel the difference in how your muscles feel as you relax?

Continue to repeat this process several times so that your forehead feels completely relaxed.

When you feel your forehead is relaxed, move on to other parts of your body.

Your jaw:
Tense the muscles in your jaw, and hold the tension for 15 seconds.

Now release the tension slowly for 30 seconds.

Once again, notice the beautiful feeling of relaxation and continue to breathe slowly. Repeat several times if needed. Your jaw can accumulate the heck of a tension!

Your neck and shoulders:

(This one is my favorite as I always accumulate lots of tension in my neck).

First, increase tension in your neck and shoulders by raising your shoulders toward your ears and hold for 15 seconds.

Slowly release the tension as you count for 30 seconds. Notice the tension gradually going away.

Your arms and hands:

Slowly draw both hands into fists. Pull your fists into your chest and hold for 15 seconds, squeezing as tight as you can. Then slowly release while you count for 30 seconds. Recognize the deep feeling of relaxation.

Your Buttocks:

Slowly increase tension in your buttocks over 15 seconds. Then, slowly release the tension over 30 seconds.

Notice the tension going away. Be sure to breathe slowly and evenly.

Your legs:

Slowly increase the tension in your quadriceps and calves over 15 seconds.

Squeeze the muscles as hard as you can. Then gently release the tension over 30 seconds. Take note of the tension leaving and embrace the feeling of relaxation.

Your Feet:

While breathing deeply and slowly, focus on increasing the tension in your feet and toes.

Now, tighten the muscles as much as you can.

Slowly release the tension while you count for 30 seconds. Notice all the stress disappearing!

Continue breathing slowly and evenly.

Do this exercise whenever you feel stressed out. The truth is- if your body is relaxed, your mind will follow. When you relax, your visualization practice will take a new dimension, and, as a bonus, you will feel great!

Relaxation can help you quickly rise above your "normal" state and reach new levels of awareness. It also blocks worry, impatience, and anxiety.

As I consciously began expanding my visualization by expanding my state throughout the day, I realized one thing.

There's always a delay in results, and we need to work on our patience.

In other words, it takes longer, at first, you may feel like you're wasting your time. This is what was happening in my mind: *why should I waste even more time to relax, if I could use it to try and write more?*

But what I learned is that thanks to visualizing and relaxing, my state improved, and so did my productivity.

I no longer felt overly attached to the end result, I could finally enjoy the process, and from there, really amazing things began manifesting in all areas of my life. It was literally like a dream come true!

Ask yourself, how do your heart, belly, and throat feel? Do you feel anxiety or any contracted energy there? Close your eyes, visualize your dream reality, always from a first-person, always through your eyes.

Take a few deep breaths. Apply the relaxation technique I shared above, whenever you notice any construction in your body, and continue your visualization.

Trust the process, hold your vision, and remember that the Universe is infinite intelligence; it already knows your order.

However, let go of your specific ways and channels you predict your desire to manifest. It may be delivered in a different way than you thought and that's OK!

The Universe may want to test you as well. Perhaps before you manifest your millions, it wants you to experience several bad investments and "failed" businesses?

Only because it wants you to practice for the bigger show so that when you finally manifest your millions, you'll know how to stay away from bad investments and business ideas. The Universe knows your path and the specific lessons you need to learn.

Don't fluctuate your state because you still can't see your dreams manifest in physical reality as fast as you wanted. Your dreams already exist, and your higher Self is already living them. So, focus your mind and heart on that! And feel good and relaxed in the present moment.

Also, take the visualization with you throughout the day. For example, when you have a look at unpaid bills, instead of worrying about them, tell yourself: *"How nice that I have access to water, energy, and internet!"*

As you pay, think about how those services help you live a comfortable life.

You get paid, let's say, it's $5000. Well, imagine it's $50000. How would you feel?

Today, focus on giving yourself the gift of relaxation, and visualize your big goal once again, to determine how it feels from your new, relaxed state.

Use the progressive relaxation technique whenever needed. A relaxed body also results in better energy, so you may find yourself manifesting some beautiful and entirely unexpected things during the day!

Let go of the baggage of stress and anxiety so that you can visualize and manifest from a genuinely relaxed place!

Chapter 5 Amplify Your Dream Vision and Achieve Your Goals Faster by Mindfully Shifting Your Identity

Now it's time for the final step. As mentioned, each chapter builds on the previous one. Now you're ready to integrate and amplify what you've learned so far!

This chapter will be especially helpful if you still feel stuck at the same level, professionally, financially, or personally. You feel like something is blocking you, even though you have the skills and the know-how to get closer to your vision.

Perhaps, you want to manifest a salary raise, and yet it's always other people in your company who get it? (Although you have more experience and expertise?). The only gap here is your energy, and we're going to fix that gap and then amplify your manifesting and visualizing abilities.

The way you're going to do this is by a massive identity shift!

It's time to visualize how to radically change your paradigm and manifest from new energy!

So how to amplify what you already have, for example, how to manifest more money? Or how to take your career to the next level and manifest a salary-raise?

Well, what do you focus on, and how do you focus on it?

What do you hold onto? Are you holding too much on your previous accomplishments and past habits and beliefs?

Maybe you work in a corporate position, but deep inside you want to start your own business. You want to follow your passion.

You've been researching and trying, but you still have this deep, many years' conditioning, this old paradigm that someone else created for you – you go to a job because it's just the way it is.

But now, you feel awakened; you are looking for something else out there, you begin to experience pain. The long commute is draining you because you're no longer passionate about your job. You feel like changing something.

Your coworkers feel like it's normal, but you feel like you don't fit in.

You know that there's a new you, new paradigm- and in this new paradigm, you're self-employed.

So now, what do you hang onto? What do your habits say?

Perhaps at the weekend, you party with corporate people, but you know you would manifest your vision fast if instead of partying on weekends, you started building your business and client base while following your soul's calling?

You mentally know the steps, but you feel your old paradigm still drives you. Change is hard!

Well, it's time to change your identity and your whole state of being, so that you can embody your vision 24/7 and easily take meaningful and inspired action to achieve your dreams with joy and ease.

Sit down. Close your eyes and take a few deep breaths. If you're not fully relaxed, do the progressive relaxation technique I shared in the previous chapter.

As soon as you start feeling relaxed, focus on visualizing your dream through the eyes of your higher-self. Envision your new Self. Your more empowered Self!

Visualize and feel in detail:

-Your thoughts – what is usually on your mind? What do you think about daily? What are the positive thoughts that drive you? What about the "problems" you may need to solve?

Please note: your New Self will also encounter some problems, but they'll be higher quality problems, your current problems will evaporate, and the "problems" that your new self might be facing now and then, will be, what your current self would give everything to experience!

Example- current problem – *I'm not making enough money to buy my dream house.*

New Self– higher quality "problem" – *I'm living in my dream house, and I can't find a good gardener.*

Example – current problem – *I can't find my dream partner.*

New Self – higher quality "problem"- *For our wedding anniversary, he wants to go to Paris, but I'd instead go to Fiji.*

-Your feelings and emotions– how do you feel when you wake up? Where do you wake up and with whom? What's around you, and what's your default feeling? Are you happy? Why are you happy? Are you waiting for something extraordinary? Are you excited? Do you feel loved and taken care of daily? Do you feel fulfilled?

-Your actions – what actions do you take when you wake up and during the day? Where do you live? What about your work? Who do you work with? Do you work from home, or do you drive to your office? What car do you drive?

-Your habits – what do you do in your free time? What do you do on weekends? What about your friends? What do they do? Who do you hang out with?

As you visualize, align yourself with your higher Self by feeling, thinking, and acting exactly as your higher-Self would.

Your manifestations always go through different stages; it's not that you can shift from one day to the next, although your conscious decision can be taken right here and right now, and you can decide to become your new identity right here and right now at this moment.

Jessica works in a corporate 9 to 5, in a good position, good salary, it's been 25 years, the job helped her support her family (as a single mom) and live comfortably. Jessica always studied LOA and was into self-development. She knew she wanted to create her own brand and give back by sharing her knowledge and helping people achieve their dreams. But she couldn't find the time. She also kept telling herself: "I can't do it now, people would think I'm a fraud, who am I to guide people to achieve their dreams if clearly, I'm not living my dream?"

So, for years, she was stuck in a cycle of excuses and limiting self-talk. She still had her passion and kept studying self-development, but her predominant thoughts were: *well, I'm not like Bob Proctor, Marie Forleo, or Tony Robbins. So, I guess nobody would listen to me anyway.*

So, she kept learning new information and growing on a mental level, but she could never take a leap of faith.

Her daughters and their education was her main focus; she wanted them to be fully independent and have great careers.

Eventually, she almost forgot about her dream of becoming a life coach.

But now, her daughters finished college and are both working and living in their own apartments. Suddenly, Jessica finds herself with not only more time, but also more money.

Jessica has been dreaming about her own coaching business for years, and at some point, she even had a few paying clients.

The results were never consistent, though, because she never thought they could be consistent. So, her thoughts, actions, and habits weren't consistent. There was no intention and no process.

So now, she wants to take the quantum leap and become a full-time coach, have her own brand, paid programs, and clients.

But...her old identity decides for her:

Hey, it's the weekend, meet your friends, and by the way, you are too old now and who would want to hire you? With so many young and tech-friendly coaches out there on social media, it would take you ages to learn. Oh, and you don't even know your exact niche, you need to nail that customer avatar first!"

So, weeks and months go by, and Jessica starts experiencing the inner struggle.

Yes, she has some clients and is grateful, but she knows she can't quit her job now because the coaching income isn't livable yet.

The only thing that can help is deep holistic visualization where you work with all your systems: your thoughts, feelings, emotions, actions, and habits.

Once again, Jessica, visualizes her dream reality where she's a successful life coach, makes a good living from her passion-based business, and has more time for her daughters, and very soon, grandchildren! Now, she has a flexible schedule and can enjoy her life while feeling fulfilled.

She asks herself: "As the new, 2.0 version of myself, how do I feel, think, and act?"

What do I think before and after talking to clients? *(Instead of continually thinking about how I suck at technology and OMG, I have no idea how market myself online!).*

No, the new Jessica thinks about what she CAN do and what she CAN master. She doesn't think negative and self-limiting thoughts.

What are her new "problems"? Well, the old problem would be: *I can't make a good living from my passion.*

The new "problem" is: *I now make an excellent income from my passion; I have a business with different streams of income. My new "problem" is that I need to hire a good accountant to help me with taxes.*

What emotions do I feel when working with clients?

Old Jessica would often feel worried, angry, frustrated and desperate, or even resentful: "*People don't want to buy from me; I attract people I don't want to serve!*"

However, new Jessica feels blessed, happy, fulfilled, and full of love because her clients are unique and a joy to work with.

In her visualization, she asks herself: *Can I keep that vibration with me in my corporate job? Let's imagine; our corporate clients are my own clients!*

As a result, she sends out this vibration to the Universe.

She now vibrates amazing energy at work and can earn more bonuses and commissions, pretty unexpectedly.

In other words, now Jessica acts from the energy of alignment, clarity, freedom, and confidence.

In her visualizations, she also focuses on her new actions.

What does the new Jessica do? What's her new work schedule as her own boss? When does she coach clients? What about doing yoga and reading in the afternoons? What about no longer feeling exhausted from that long commute?

It all starts in her mind! Jessica gets clear on what she wants (not what the society wants), and she practices being receptive to new thoughts, feelings, actions, and emotions.

She realizes she was too stuck in the how, precisely, the negative how (how she could not live her dream life and do her passion for a living).

So, Jessica decides to experiment with her new, empowered version where she's a full-time coach, so that she can shift her identity.

Using holistic visualization every morning and every evening while practicing gratitude and tricking her mind during the day whenever she could *(for example, after getting a business inquiry, she imagined she was getting dozens and she felt the joy immediately!)*.

Suddenly, the "how" began manifesting itself, and it turned out she could be a successful coach without having to be a technology wizard.

Jessica began organizing local events and local client groups, which led to a steady income.

She quit her job, and found herself with more free time. Then, she could finally take a portion of her business online and learn new skills and online marketing (she used to fear so much!) with joy and ease.

As a new person, she began thinking differently, all because she visualized every day to expand her mindset.

Old Jessica felt scared of investing money in her business. She felt OK spending much more on expensive dinners and clothes she didn't need but felt scared to invest in a good coach and mentor for herself.

New Jessica feels whole and complete. As a result, she shifts her focus. Old Jessica felt scared of technology and running an online business, but new Jessica, acts with conviction, hiring experts who could help her grow online so that she could focus on what she was good at – serving clients.

What was once an excuse or a negative how, got solved by her new, more empowered, 2.0 version of herself.

So, check your alignment...Are you acting in favor of or against your new self and your dreams? Are you still confined to your old emotions, energy, actions, and thoughts?

Are you holding onto your old self and old patterns?

All personal development books say that growth comes from leaving your comfort zone while having deep faith. It's time to apply this gem into our lives!

Well, it all starts in your mind, so visualization is your best friend on this journey because you can experiment with and experience new realities and even pick and choose between them. Remember, it's like trying out some new clothes. If you find something you like, take it and wear it!

Mindful visualization can even help you save years of chasing your own tail and doing things you hate.

By experiencing your new reality through visualization, you slowly start experiencing your new self, with new thoughts, feelings, emotions, and actions.

And your new self has got all the answers- however, it'll want you to think, feel and act in alignment with who you are becoming, not necessarily with who you are now (unless who you, right now is already aligned with your dream reality).

The best way to experience a paradigm shift is via visualization.

You don't have to worry about destroying the old paradigm.

Instead, focus on adding! Yes, focus on adding new elements to your reality through visualization, and the new paradigm will come in on autopilot. Allow all your cells to feel familiar with your new reality.

The reason why people get stuck on the same level is because there is no alignment between their actions, thoughts, and feelings. They desire something intellectually, but their feelings, actions, and emotions don't follow.

For example, a person visualizes their dream reality and financial abundance, but then they see a book or a course that can teach them something to get closer to their goals, and they say *no* because they're too scared to invest in themselves.

A person visualizes a fulfilling career and a passion-based business. Still, then, when the opportunity arises, instead of dedicating some time to mastering their craft, they escape to watching TV, thinking that it's too late for them to learn something new.

Remember, it's never too late to pursue your goals. So, never blame yourself and never dwell on "lost opportunities." They aren't lost; if anything, they're much better now, because you're a totally different person!

Go through this book several times and let the information sink in. Mindfully practice each step so that you can create your own visualization system that feels good for you and serves you for years to come.

I believe in you; whenever you feel lonely on your journey, remember that you're an incredible, highly vibrating being, destined to live in health, love, wealth, happiness, and abundance of whatever you desire.

Manifesting a new reality can be a bit like going through a dark tunnel sometimes, but remember there's a light at the end of that tunnel! So, always focus on that light and be that light!

Now, that you know how to work in alignment and how to use visualization holistically while integrating all your systems, you have everything you need to create your own reality!

The following pages contain a couple of bonus tips and advanced manifestation techniques that I believe can be very helpful for you so that you can take your visualizations and manifestations to the next level. Enjoy and happy manifesti

Bonus Exercise: Are You Blocking Unexpected Channels of Money, Abundance, and Love?

What if I told you that most of the time, we subconsciously or even consciously block new channels of abundance?

When I say "abundance," I mean not only money but also: happy moments, energy, health, and even love.

But, for the sake of this chapter, let's use money as an example.

The interesting part is that we all tend to do this, and I also caught myself blocking new channels of abundance, by being too stuck in my "normal ways" (and by being too logical as well!).

The best way to explain how we often block ourselves from receiving our wishes is to give you different examples, such as:

1. In the LOA community, many people get fixated on manifesting money through winning the lottery, as if it was the ONLY way. Heck, some people even think that LOA is and has to be about winning the lottery; and if it's not, then it doesn't work.

Such thinking blocks other channels of creative self-expression or other channels of unexpected abundance. A person may consciously reject a new project at work, or learning a new high-income skill, or pursuing a passion that can result in abundance at some point in their lives (or get them on a new path).

2. Some people think of manifesting money, and the ONLY way they believe they can do this is by getting a salary raise or a new job. Again, nothing wrong with that, I'm all for ambition, if it's genuinely coming from your heart.

But...abundance could also come from an investment, a side project/business, or something completely different, that your mind doesn't even know yet (but your higher Self does!).

3. In my case, since I've been running different online businesses for years, I used to think that the only way to manifest more abundance was by setting up some other business venture in the online space.

So, I got stuck in creating online assets and chasing passive income. I was learning from different business authors. While I'm very grateful for the skills and knowledge I gained from their work, a part of me closed itself to other channels of receiving abundance.

I was getting too logical, and at some point, I'd struggle to take inspired action on new ideas that would come to my mind, because I'd over-analyze each idea using the metrics I formerly learned from business authors.

Oh, is it an asset or a liability? Will it give me the freedom of time and location? Will it violate the business commandments that one of the authors I read talked about?

Once again, I'm very grateful for everything I learned, both from spirituality and business leaders. It's all useful information.

And everyone is on a different journey; there's no right or wrong. What matters is what's good for you NOW. It's the NOW that can transform our lives, so why block it?

The bottom line is- we need to be OPEN to the unexpected and take INSPIRED action on the ideas that come from our intuition, without over-analyzing them and without using other people's way of thinking (yes, learn from experts but think for yourself).

We need to let go of the attachment and take new actions, in new fields, all from a place of love and curiosity.

Imagine a little child learning how to walk. The toddler just keeps learning, falling, and getting up, without analyzing each step.

So, how did I open myself to new channels of manifesting abundance and how you can do it too?

Well, start with an exciting vision.

Visualize your ideal day in your dream life. Don't overthink how it'll happen. Just allow it to be and feel it in your mind's eye, your soul, and all your body.

Do this twice a day and aim for a deeply relaxed state as you do this.

After you finish this exercise, set an intention to the Universe (think or say it out loud):

I'm open to manifesting abundance from new, unexpected channels. I'm open to growth and expansion. I'm open to venturing into the unknown.

After a few weeks into doing this exercise, I manifested:

-an unexpected and pretty unusual deal from an audio book company (after 3 years of writing and publishing, one email and call changed my entire year!)

-very inexpensive, practically "symbolic" rent in a lovely beach house (a friend of a friend was going traveling, and wanted someone with "good energy" and a love for cats to take care of his home)

-many unexpected discounts and coupons (you see, the old me would rudely label them as some "cheapskate stuff" and so, I was blocking myself from receiving anything new and probably blocking many other things)

-increased energy and vitality, which allowed me to read and study new skills very fast and start new services based on my new skills!

-amazing furniture for my parents (a friend was moving houses and offered me his furniture which I could not take, so I asked my parents, turned out, they were saving money for new furniture, so they were excited to get it for free, save money and use it for a well-deserved vacation instead!)

-increased creativity that allows me to write more and attract amazing readers like You!

-amazing LOA success stories for my friends and readers

One thing I had to be very mindful of was taking inspired action on new ideas, even if they seemed weird and not connected to my "logical plan".

Well, your higher Self knows!

To sum up:

1. Be grateful for all your current manifestation channels such as a job, clients, business, side-hustle, tax return.
2. Visualize your dream life and perfect day - daily without logically thinking about the HOW.
3. Throughout the day, be grateful for all the big and little things and use positive language (to yourself and others)
4. Take inspired action on new ideas from a place of love, fun, and curiosity.
5. Keep affirming that you're completely open to new channels of receiving abundance.
6. Act accordingly to that intention. For example, if you want to manifest a loving partner, and until now you thought that the only way to do so is via online dating, and then a friend calls you with a free invitation to a yoga class, just go there! Maybe the Universe wants you to meet someone there, or at least get you on some new path that will eventually lead to you meeting your dream partner.

If you want to manifest abundance, and a friend suggests you read some business book, act on it. You never know, maybe just one idea in that book, will open a new gate for you? Even if you never even thought you were into running your own business.

Always be open to learning, growing, and expanding!

Bonus Tip: How Not to Visualize

When visualizing, the main intention should be to release resistance, not to create more of it. The good thing is that when you visualize, your brain is getting primed in a compelling way while creating reference experiences, right now in the present moment.

This practice works excellent for re-programming your subconscious mind. As with all the manifestation techniques, you need the feeling you can align with your mind and heart, too!

The most common mistake people make when visualizing is that they see themselves in a movie, from a third person. What it does is that you don't identify yourself with it, and it's harder to manifest. You're separating yourself rather than fusing yourself with your vision.

It's much better to imagine it through your eyes.

Also, visualization is not about some external point in the future. You have the power to make yourself feel any emotion you want right here right now. Visualize things that make you feel good, feel proud of yourself. Visualizing the process is also very powerful – so practice your new, empowered version.

Fuse yourself with it to practice your unique vibration and align yourself with it.

Stay in that vibration in your everyday activities. Your old apartment can be treated like your own villa if you regard it as such. When you check your bank account and see, let's say

$2000, imagine it's $20,000, or $200,000. Imagine it's there, and it's safe, you're safe. It's normal for you to make, keep, spend, and invest money. Money always comes to you, and it replenishes easily. Money likes you.

If you want to manifest a healthy, fit body, and you run one mile a day, imagine you can run five or even ten miles! In other words, use everyday routines and situations to trick your brain into thinking:

It's already happening, and it's something normal for me! Imagine a person whose desire is to be a well-known stand-up comedian who gets a small local gig, but there are only 30 people in the audience. But, the person can choose to pretend that there are 300 people or even 3,000 people, why not? Another person wants to lose 20 pounds and already lost 2 pounds. Well, they can pretend they've lost 10 or 12 pounds already!

Your brain is a machine that loves getting clear signals. Communicate with it through emotions and visualizations. Your brain LOVES such games!

Question:
I struggle with visualizing from the first person, but I'm working hard to change that already :) I want to manifest a six-figure position in my company. I'm very close as I recently got a significant promotion.

I've been following your books and emails for a few months now, and they empowered me. I know that LOA works, and a recent promotion (even though it's still not my big goal) feels like the first step on my manifestation journey.

So, I want to keep practicing visualization. I try to focus on my new office, new business meetings, but it's a bit blurry, and I can't fully feel it. Any tips to make it easier and faster with my visualization?

Answer:
The best tip is to focus on the things you love doing. Seriously! You need to ask yourself why you intend to manifest that six-figure job. What drives you?

Is it the prestige and recognition at your company? Your dedication and hard work? If yes, keep visualizing the work you'd do and focus on the process and how you enjoy it. If however, your desire to manifest a six-figure salary is because you want to improve your lifestyle, focus on the freedom the money can give you.

For example, exotic travels, shopping, eating at nice restaurants. How would you think as a six-figure earner? How would you manage your money? Would you invest? Would you have an accountant? Again, there's no reason to overthink if it makes you feel confused. Stick to the questions that make you feel good, and excited and use them as a foundation for your visualizations. Whatever makes you feel good!

Question:
Can you teach me how to stop thinking about someone all the time? That person is draining my energy. I try not to, but I still think about him, and I hate it. I want to let go of that person and move on.

Answer:
Practise meditation. You won't believe me, but I was just like you. I, too used to overthink and could not let go. Relax. Meditate. Visualize you are all by yourself in beautiful locations. It always works! Also, don't get too caught up in trying. Focus more on mindful visualization.

Question:
There are many opportunities I'd like to manifest to become a multi-entrepreneur, with different streams of income, but I'm not so sure which one I should pick first. I assume it's better to manifest one specific thing and only then do something else? So, how do I begin visualizing? Should I start from the most lucrative opportunity?

Answer:

Focus more on what you are passionate about, and then those things will all come as a side effect. Money is a side-effect of us doing our passion while being of service to others etc.

For example, several years ago, I'd visualize myself doing videos and selling expensive programs and retreats. I thought it was the only way because I saw other people manifest abundance doing it.

However, I had no passion for it at all. I'm a writer at my core, and this is my authentic self. I spent about three years, visualizing what was not for me to begin with.

As a result, I could never get it. The Universe kindly refused because it wasn't for me; there was a much better path for me. So, if visualization doesn't work for you now, it can also mean you aren't passionate about what you want, and something better, much better, will unfold for you. So, you can't lose my friend; you can only win!

#3 Your mind works like a search engine, use it wisely to find your dreams!

Your mind works like a search engine. So, if you are always thinking about your fears and the worst-case scenarios, your mind will show you even more negative situations. Your mind loves those negative "upsells"!. Take it, here is one more negative scene for you, I know you love this stuff!

Lately, I have been looking into working with a mentor, I heard lots of good things about him. So I googled his company and added "success stories" to it because I was looking for inspiration. I wanted to see how other people transformed using his teachings.

At the same time, one of my friends, who is a bit more skeptical, google his name and added "scam" to it.

Nothing wrong with that, you can google whatever you want. And whatever it is that you focus on- your mind will find the evidence for it.

So, in my case, I found the information that the company and the programs are legit. And I got inspired by people who used those programs and reached out for more information.

However, my friend assumed it was not a legitimate company and forced herself to prove her thoughts right. Once again- nothing wrong with that. In some cases, it's good to be skeptical, and I am not saying that you should always believe everyone and what they say. Do your due diligence.

What I want to draw your attention to is that your mind is like a google search engine.

Let's say you work in sales. Or you are making sales to grow your own business. If in your mind, you assume that you love talking to people, and that you are doing them a big favor by making them offers, you always attract great clients, it's normal for you, and your mind will align you with the evidence and actions that will make your life easier.

However, if your mind goes like:

Oh no... What if I get on the phone with them and in the end, I will share my price and they will tell me it's too much?

And what if we work together and I don't deliver results?

What if they post a negative review about me?

What, if, what if...and only the negative.

So, from now on, whenever you catch yourself in those negative what if's, accept them (don't judge yourself for having them).

Examples of asking empowering questions and doing positive searches:

What if I call this prospect now and they buy? What would it feel like?

What if I apply for that job, and I get it? What would it feel like?

What if I work less and make more money? What would it feel like?

BTW, you can also use this love-based mindset (aka your mind is a search engine technique) to improve other areas of life.

What if I go on this diet and I love it?

What if I drink those smoothies every day, and my skin looks great?

What if I stop drinking and still have fun while going out?

So, this is the first step. Switch your mindset from fear-based to love-based. Picture the image in your mind and really feel it. Loved-based mindset will connect you with the right ideas, it will guide you. It will propel you to take purposeful and inspired action in alignment with your vision.

Whenever you meditate, focus on your thoughts and let them be. If you catch any negative thoughts trying to get you off track, be sure to re-write them to positive thoughts.

You can google yourself with a "success story" at the end of the search phrase. Or, you can google yourself with "why it didn't work." It's up to you.

And the funny thing is, whatever you focus on, your mind will find the evidence in its search engine...

So, want kind of evidence will you be looking for?

Conclusion

The law of attraction is the real phenomena, and you'll find millions upon millions of law of attraction success stories.

At the same time, many people give up because it didn't work for them right away, or they came across some subconscious blocks (whether they knew it or not).

What's of paramount importance is your perception. See the LOA and manifestation process as a long-term tool to help you align with your higher self and embrace positivity for good.

Use it to focus on your energy, health, and happiness while letting go of old fears and doubts. Grow your manifestation muscle.

The Universe might be sending you some obstacles here and there to make you leave your comfort zone or re-align your path so that you can manifest your vision and create long-term success in all areas of your life.

You're reading this book and its final pages for a reason. Never limit your dreams because of some initial setbacks.

The Universe is just testing you and giving you some fantastic tools for you to grow.

Just tune in and listen. Stay strong, my friend! I hope we "meet" again in another book.

Remember - I love you, I believe in you, and I pray for you!

Thank you for reading this little book until the very end! Now, before you go, I'd love your feedback!

So, if you have any thoughts to share about this book, please post a review on Amazon and Good Reads.

It doesn't have to be long if you're busy; in fact, just one sentence will do.

Please let us know the number one lesson you got from this book and who you think could benefit from reading it.

Your review can help other readers in our community, unleash the power of visualization and get closer to their dreams.

I love hearing from my readers, and I'm eager to read your review.

Thank You, and have a beautiful day!

PS. To stay in touch with me, my latest author updates and new releases, follow my website and my Amazon page at:

www.LOAforSuccess.com

www.amazon.com/author/elenagrivers

Until next time, much love!

Your friend and mentor in mindful LOA & manifestation!

Free LOA Newsletter + Bonus Gift

To help you AMPLIFY what you've learned in this book, I'd like to offer you a free copy of my ***LOA Workbook – a powerful, FREE 5-day program (eBook & audio)*** designed to help you raise your vibration while eliminating resistance and negativity.

To sign up for free, visit the link below now:

www.loaforsuccess.com/newsletter

You'll also get free access to my highly acclaimed, uplifting **LOA Newsletter.**

Through this email newsletter, I regularly share all you need to know about the manifestation mindset and energy.

My newsletter alone helped hundreds of my readers manifest their own desires.

Plus, whenever I release a new book, you can get it at a deeply discounted price or even for free.

You can also start receiving my new audiobooks published on Audible at no cost!

To sign up for free, visit the link below now:

www.loaforsuccess.com/newsletter

I'd love to connect with you and stay in touch with you while helping you on your LOA journey!

If you happen to have any technical issues with your sign up, please email us at:

support@LOAforSuccess.com

About Elena G.Rivers

Elena G. Rivers is a bestselling author with a passion for writing highly uplifting Law of Attraction and spiritual self-help books aimed at helping ambitious souls manifest their dream reality.

Her tools are practical and effective; she's a big believer in simplicity. What separates Elena from most LOA "gurus" is that instead of chasing the latest "manifestation method," Elena focuses on tested exercises to help you permanently shift your mindset and energy to create a new, more empowered version of yourself and mindfully create a life you love.

She fuses her proven manifestation tools with deep inner work to help you embrace self-love and transform your self-image in a powerful way. After all, you don't attract what you want; instead, you attract who you are - this is the real LOA work and profound metamorphosis you can experience by reading one of Elena's books!

Please note that Elena's books are aimed at ambitious souls – people who are committed to doing the inner work and transforming on a deeper level. She writes mostly for powerful creators, heart-led entrepreneurs, leaders, professionals, creatives, empaths, and healers – people who desire to manifest abundance by creating value in the world.

Her work is NOT for people looking for quick shortcuts, instant lottery wins, and easy fixes without even trying to change their mindset, skills, and energy.

However, if you're ready to launch a new, more empowered version of yourself, eliminate negativity, and raise your vibration to manifest your dream reality based on who you're becoming- you're in for a spiritual treat!

Elena's books combine the metaphysical with the practical, to help you, a busy and ambitious 21st century person, manifest with joy and ease. She also fills her books with real life success stories of people who enriched their lives with LOA- to help you stay inspired and flourish in a high vibration.

When not writing, Elena enjoys indulging in self-care, meditating, yoga, reading, traveling, long walks in nature, listening to audiobooks, and inspirational programs, cooking, and eating.

She loves connecting with her readers and serving them on a deeper level, so feel free to join her email newsletter to say hi, receive free lessons, and share your thoughts, offer suggestions, and deliver feedback:

www.loaforsuccess.com/newsletter

More Books by Elena G.Rivers

Available on Amazon – eBook, paperback and hardcover editions are not available for your convenience

(just search for "Elena G.Rivers" in your local Amazon Store) For more information and direct links to our books, visit the author's website at:

www.LOAforSuccess.com

The Money Mindset Audiobook is now available on Audible! For more information, visit:

www.LOAforSuccess.com/audiobooks

How NOT to Manifest (Law of Attraction Short Reads Book 2)

Be sure to check out Elena bestselling book: "How NOT to Manifest" -now available on Amazon (eBook, paperback and hardcover editions are available for your convenience)

Are You Ready to Discover the Hidden Law of Attraction Mistakes That Are Blocking You from Manifesting Your Dream Reality?

Do you want to manifest with ease and confidence?

If the answer is yes, you've arrived at the right place!

How Not to Manifest is designed to help you identify your MANIFESTATION BLOCKS, so that you can create a life full of happiness, abundance, and love.

You see, it's NOT only about the manifestation methods you use.

In reality, the true secret to success resides in your energy, VIBRATION, and mindset. You don't attract what you want; you attract WHO you are.

By permanently SHIFTING your mindset and energy, you automatically align yourself with your true desires and manifest them into your reality.

Are you ready for a full transformation without hoping, dreaming, and trying?

The information you'll discover in this book works both for LOA beginners and for seasoned "manifestors" who want to take it to the next level!

You'll find all you need to know to quickly identify your MANIFESTATION MISTAKES and correct them to manifest with joy, empowerment, and ease!

♥ Here's Exactly What You'll Discover ***Inside How Not To Manifest*** ♥:

- The LOA DETECTIVE Exercise to quickly spot your hidden feelings and emotions that BLOCK your manifestations

-The Reverse Engineer "Recipe" to help you ALIGN with the manifestation methods that work MAGIC for you!

-Tips to assist if you can never manifest the big things, only the small things

-Examples and EVIDENCE why releasing the fear of failure isn't enough and the biggest Manifestation Enemy that may be holding you back from living full potential (LOA gurus don't want you to know this!)

-The On-Demand Deep Healing method to RELEASE NEGATIVITY once and for all

-How NOT to visualize - the visualization MISTAKES that can make you manifest what you don't want (and what to do instead)

-The TOXIC words you must stop using and the MAGNETIC words to use instead (works like magic!)

-The Deadly LOA Sin and scripting mistake that made me lose THOUSANDS of dollars (and how I corrected it to manifest abundance and happiness)

-The SHOCKING truth: why some people succeed with LOA without affirmations, vision boards, visualizations, or scripting

-NATURAL remedies and holistic techniques to release stress, anxiety, insomnia, and RESISTANCE

-The Manifestation Habit Stacking method to instantly raise your VIBRATION without any complicated rituals

***

The TRUTH is – the law of attraction always works!

But, if you don't shift your mindset and energy, it'll likely not work for your advantage.

Life is too short to waste on things that don't attract what you DESIRE.

So, if you're ready to LET GO of old habits, mindsets, and energies that are holding you back from manifesting your dream life,

order your copy of "How NOT to Manifest" now from Amazon, or go to: www.LOAforSuccess.com

♥ Join thousands of others who are using this life-changing power and make LOA work for you, once and for all! ♥

"Lots of Law of Attraction books focus on what you're supposed to be doing but they never share the things we shouldn't. And with the LOA, it's important that the total mind be focused on manifestation, not cluttered with things that are blocking the positioned you need to successfully manifest. This book provides solid advice on things to avoid, clearing your energies of negative thought and helping being about the good things you're trying to bring into your life. An easy read that will change your LOA thoughts immediately."
– by Stephanie, US

"This book was instrumental in a spiritual shift I have been trying to implement. I have been stuck for a while and I had two huge a-ha moments while reading. This book is so full of "wisdom nuggets" it is now my go to book when I am stuck financially, spiritually and energetically. Thank you Elena!"
– by Jo, US

CPSIA information can be obtained
at www.ICGtesting.com
Printed in the USA
BVHW051401281021
620172BV00002B/139

9 781800 950481